Keep Your Eye On
AMANDA!

Keep Your Eye On AMANDA!

Illustrated by
David Wisniewski

AN AVON CAMELOT BOOK

Keep Your Eye On Amanda! originally appeared in serial form in various newspapers in the United States and Canada.

AVON BOOKS, INC.
1350 Avenue of the Americas
New York, New York 10019

A Note from Avi copyright © 1999 by Avi
Text copyright © 1996, 1997 by Avi
Illustrations copyright © 1999 by David Wisniewski
Published by arrangement with the author
Visit our website at **http://www.AvonBooks.com**
Library of Congress Catalog Card Number: 98-93059
ISBN: 0-380-80337-2

First Avon Camelot Printing: February 1999

CAMELOT TRADEMARK REG. U.S. PAT. OFF. AND IN OTHER COUNTRIES, MARCA REGISTRADA, HECHO EN U.S.A.

Printed in the U.S.A.

OPM   10   9   8   7   6   5   4   3   2   1

Contents

A Note from Avi

As I grew up in New York City in the 1940s, newspapers were important in my household. On weekdays we had a morning paper as well as an afternoon paper. The Sunday papers were big, bulky, but endlessly fascinating. I always started my day reading the sports section. I still do.

One newspaper, the *New York Herald Tribune*, carried animal stories by Thorton W. Burgess. In his time Burgess wrote many, many volumes for children, most of them serialized in daily papers. Such serial tales had been common in newspapers and magazines for about a hundred years. It was only with the advent of TV after the end of World War II that these stories ceased to be printed.

Not only did I read these tales by Burgess in the

newspaper, they became the first books I bought with my own money. I think they cost fifty cents a hardbound volume.

As I grew older I remembered those stories fondly. I even nursed the idea that I would like to try my hand at a serialized novel. Perhaps I could revive the format.

One night in 1996, when living in Boulder, Colorado, I was visited by a pair of raccoons. It was that which led to my writing *Keep Your Eye On Amanda!* On October 3, 1996, the Colorado Springs *Gazette Telegraph* began to publish the story over a period of twenty-one weeks. In time more than eighty newspapers around the country published the book, reaching some nine million readers. The first *Amanda* book was followed by *Amanda Joins the Circus.*

Since then I have founded a foundation called Breakfast Serials. Its mission is to bring good writing and illustrators to today's kids in today's newspapers.

Chapter One

PHILIP AND AMANDA

"But I don't want to be a thief," said Philip, a plump and very anxious young raccoon. He was staring at a two-story brick building across Grove Street, through a light veil of powdery snow. It was a little past three o'clock in the morning in Boulder, Colorado.

Amanda, Philip's twin sister, rolled her eyes. "You're such a dork!" she said. Amanda was smaller and thinner than Philip with a narrow, sharp-nosed, white-whiskered face. The black band across her eyes gave her the appearance of a thief. "Live a little!" she said. "It's no big deal to go inside a house."

"I'm not so sure," Philip replied. His round ears twitched as he rubbed his front paws together with worry.

Annoyed by her brother's reluctance, Amanda said,

1

"Philip, I watched the people move out two days ago. And I didn't see anyone move in." She flicked snow from her nose.

Philip studied his twin with troubled eyes. "But you weren't watching *all* the time, were you?"

"Now you're being *stupid!*" Amanda said with exasperation. "Does it *look* like anyone is in there?"

"But if no one's there," Philip suggested, "what's the point of going in? There won't be any food."

"People *always* leave stuff behind. It'll be awesome. Anyway, I'm bored. And you are hungry, aren't you?"

Philip sighed. His sister was right. He *was* hungry, and maybe there would be food. And the house appeared deserted. Its windows were dark. No curtains were in sight. There was not so much as a curl of smoke coming from the chimney on the roof.

What's more, the house did look as if getting inside would be easy. Next to the porch was a pine tree which reached the porch roof and beyond. Overlooking the porch roof was a partially open window. The house was almost inviting them to enter!

Even so, Philip felt uneasy about going in. How he wished he was snug and safe at home.

"Ma said we shouldn't go into people's houses," he reminded his sister.

"Hey, dude, how old is Ma?"

"Ten, I think."

"Exactly. Like, too old to know anything," Amanda insisted. "Know what I'm saying? Besides, eating food that's been left behind is not stealing."

"But what if there isn't any food?" Philip asked.

"No food, no me, no problem."

As Philip stared at the building he thought how vague Amanda was about right and wrong. He knew it was wrong to go into people's houses. Still, wasn't their mother always saying, "Philip, keep your eye on Amanda! She loves excitement too much." He *had* to go with her.

"Philip," Amanda said sarcastically, "be a wuss if you want. I'm going in." So saying, she scampered across Grove Street, leaving a double row of five-toed paw prints in the new snow.

Philip watched her with a heavy heart. He just knew she was going to get into trouble.

"Are you coming?" Amanda called from the far side.

Philip looked up and down the street. Seeing no cars, he waddled slowly and reluctantly toward the house.

Amanda, already on the porch, stood on her hind legs and peeked into the house through a large window. The moonlight illuminated a long room. Other than a few scattered boxes and a broom against a wall, it appeared completely empty.

"See," Amanda cooed. "Like, it's *so* sweet. No one's there."

Philip looked for himself. The house certainly did seem abandoned. "Amanda, isn't it wrong to—" He stopped speaking. Amanda was halfway up the tree. With an inward groan, Philip followed.

Once on the porch roof, Amanda climbed to the sill of the open window. A block of wood held it open.

Not even bothering to see if Philip was following, she crept through the gap into the house.

Philip, now on the porch roof, hesitated. What was he to do? Should *he* do something wrong to keep Amanda from doing wrong? Once again he remembered his mother saying that she expected him to keep an eye on Amanda. With that, Philip followed his sister inside. His heart was pounding.

Fatter than Amanda, he found it a tight squeeze. Still, he managed to get through and drop onto a rug-covered floor, just in time to hear Amanda say, "Oh, bummer! Someone *is* here."

[NEXT WEEK: TRAPPED!]

Chapter Two

TRAPPED!

Using his bushy tail to keep steady, a frightened Philip sat up on his hind legs. Across the room a man lay asleep on a bed. He was fully dressed, but snoring. "What—what do we do now?" Philip stammered.

"Hey," Amanda said, "as long as he doesn't hear us we're cool."

"Cool?" Philip fairly gagged with panic. "Amanda, people catch raccoons! Cage them! Skin them! Eat them! I don't think we should stay here."

"You can go home if you want," Amanda said.

Philip, feeling positively ill, shrank down.

"I'm going downstairs," Amanda said smugly. "You'll see, there'll be plenty of food below." She hurried away.

Philip went to the stairwell and peered down after her. When he saw it was a spiral staircase his stomach

6

churned. "This is a disaster," he murmured to himself, even as he forced himself to descend.

The corkscrew twist of the steps made him dizzy. Twice he had to stop. By the time he reached the first floor he was very wobbly.

He looked about, noting the boxes as well as an empty fireplace.

"Philip!" he heard Amanda cry. "Come here! Quick!"

Hoping his sister had decided to leave, Philip scurried across the smooth wooden floor into the kitchen. It had a small refrigerator, stove, sink, counters, and cabinets, plus a stool next to the counter.

"Have you decided to go?" Philip asked.

"Like, totally awesome!" Amanda cried, ignoring the question. Nearby sat an open paper sack labeled DOG FOOD. In the palm of her paw was a heap of brown pellets.

"Didn't I tell you it would be worth it?" Amanda cried. She gobbled the pellets and grabbed some more. "Be better if I wet it," she said. "Ah, cool," she cooed, "a bathroom."

Sure enough, next to the kitchen was a bathroom with a sink, a toilet, and a large tub standing on claw feet. "Water," Amanda announced. She lifted the toilet seat, washed her food, ate some more pellets, then hurried back to the kitchen. Snatching up more dog food, she returned to the bathroom.

A hungry Philip went to the dog food and cautiously tried a few pellets. "Phooey!" To him the food tasted like old fungus. Then he lifted his nose and sniffed. The scent of something wonderfully delicious filled his nose.

He took a step in one direction. The smell lessened. He moved another way and it intensified. Following his nose, Philip crossed the room, only to bump against a counter. He looked up. On top of the counter were a few boxes, an open bottle of peanut oil, and a bag labeled GRANOLA.

Granola. Philip almost swooned. Granola meant toasted oats, rice bits, raisins, maybe even nuts. Philip loved nuts. Using the stool rungs as a ladder, he quickly reached the counter. Once there, he paused, suddenly remembering the man upstairs. Since there was a person around wasn't taking the food wrong? Well, maybe, he thought, it had been left by the people who moved out. Besides, he was very hungry.

Unable to resist, Philip opened the bag, plunged his nose inside, and took a deep sniff. "Stale nuts," he murmured with joy. "Awesome!"

As Philip stuffed his mouth, his tail swished with so much excitement he knocked the oil bottle off the counter. With a loud crash it hit the floor. Oil gushed everywhere.

"What's happening?" Amanda called from the bathroom.

"Nothing. Just a bottle," Philip managed to say. His mouth was too full to say more.

Amanda returned to the dog food while Philip kept grabbing pawfulls of granola, filling his mouth as fast as he could.

Suddenly, a light flashed on from upstairs, followed by the sound of someone descending the spiral steps.

Both Philip and Amanda froze.

"Is that someone there?" called a man's voice. "I'm coming down!"

[NEXT WEEK: THE MAN IN THE HOUSE]

THE STORY SO FAR:

AMANDA AND PHILIP, TWIN RACCOONS, ARE STEALING
FOOD FROM A HOUSE IN BOULDER, COLORADO,
ONLY TO BE DISCOVERED BY A MAN.

Chapter Three

THE MAN IN THE HOUSE

Hearing the man descend the stairs, Amanda bolted back into the bathroom. Philip, meanwhile, leaped off the counter onto the floor. With a splat, he hit the puddle of peanut oil and skidded into the big room with the fireplace—exactly where he did not want to be. As the person reached the first floor, Philip dove behind a box. It was just in time. Peeking out he saw a man in a dapper brown suit and necktie as well as sunglasses which looked like a mask. Philip gasped: At first glance the man looked like an enormous raccoon.

Terrified, Philip watched as the man stepped into the kitchen. "Well, I'll be!" Philip heard him say. "Looks like I've been visited by thieves!" The next moment there was an awful crash. The man had slipped on the oil.

Philip panicked. He tore up the spiral staircase, trying

to reach the window through which they'd entered. To his horror it was shut. The bit of wood holding it open lay on the floor. When he'd crawled through, he had knocked it out.

Hearing the man coming back upstairs, Philip flung himself under the bed.

The man pulled on his shoes. "Thieves," he muttered. "Of all the rotten luck. Just when I was about to go to work. I better take care of them first."

Fearing for his life, Philip shot out from beneath the bed and plunged down the steps, going so fast he tripped and somersaulted the last spiral.

"Stop! Come back!" the man shouted after him.

Woozy but panicky, Philip dashed from window to window in the desperate hope that one would be open. None were. Skidding and sliding, he shot into the bathroom and hurled himself under the bathtub where Amanda was hiding. She was popping dog food pellets into her mouth.

"It's a man!" Philip panted. "And he's after us."

"Hey! No problem," Amanda said calmly. "Like, I can talk myself out of anything."

"But what about me?" Philip cried, pressing as close to his sister as possible.

Amanda rolled her eyes. "Chill, Philip, chill!"

"Chill?" Philip screeched. "Amanda, he's going to catch us. Kill us! Cook us or—"

"Philip," Amanda barked, "calm yourself!"

The man was coming back. From the sound of his tread, the raccoons were certain he was in the kitchen.

He stopped. Then he began to move toward the bathroom.

"Amanda . . ." Philip pleaded in a whisper.

"Let me handle this, dude!" she replied.

Philip squeezed behind his sister and covered his eyes with his paws. As for Amanda, she kept her eyes focused on the man's shoes.

The man entered the bathroom, paused, then peered under the tub. "Ah! There you are!" he said and hurried out of the room.

"Where's he going?" Philip asked in a quavering voice.

"Probably running away," Amanda said with a giggle.

But the next moment the man returned. This time he stuck a broom under the tub and shoved it right at the two raccoons. "Go away, thieves!" he called. "Get!"

"Look out!" Philip warned.

"Ouch!" Amanda cried as the broom struck her paw.

Giving way to his terror, Philip cried, "Amanda! Run for it." Almost blind with panic, Philip burst from under the tub, crashing into the man's legs so hard the man tumbled over.

"Help!" the man cried. "I'm being attacked!"

Philip, scrambling faster than ever, careened madly through the kitchen toward the spiral steps. As he neared them he realized the man had opened the front door. With a burst of energy Philip all but flew out of the house, onto the porch, and into the snow, landing chin-first. Behind him the front door slammed shut.

"We made it," he panted, and turned to where he

assumed Amanda would be. But his sister was not there. Only then did Philip realize she was still inside the house.

[NEXT WEEK: WHAT HAPPENED TO AMANDA?]

THE STORY SO FAR:

WHEN HER BROTHER PHILIP ESCAPES FROM THE HOUSE,
AMANDA IS LEFT BEHIND TO FEND FOR HERSELF.

Chapter Four

WHAT HAPPENED
TO AMANDA?

Staggering out from beneath the tub, Amanda threw herself on the floor. "I've been endangered!" she shrieked. To prove it she rolled onto her back and stuck her four feet stiffly into the air. "It's all because I'm starving and needed a bit to eat on a freezing winter's night," she wailed. "Oh, my poor old mother was right."

"Right about what?" asked the man with the sunglasses.

"I've been a wild, thoughtless raccoon," Amanda wept. "I deserve to suffer and be in pain!"

"Are you hurting a great deal?" the man asked.

Amanda wiggled one of her paws. "Yes," she whimpered.

"I thought you were robbing me," the man said.

"Hey, man, no way," Amanda said. "I just wanted some food to bring to my mom." Again the tears flowed.

"If you'd just asked," the man offered, "you could have helped yourself. This isn't my food."

Amanda stopped her tears and looked around. "What do you mean? Don't you live here?"

"Not really," the man said. "I'm just putting the house to good use. And by the way, my name is Joe."

Amanda sat up and considered Joe. He was a slim, trim fellow, with a crest of brown hair. His eyes, as seen through his sunglasses, were dark. Cool, she thought.

"I believe," explained Joe, "that houses are meant to be lived in. An empty one makes me feel so sad I move right in. I only do it to make the house feel better."

Amanda smiled slyly. "I like the way you think, man. And you can call me Mandy."

"Now, Mandy, were you trying to steal food from me?"

"No way," replied Amanda earnestly. "I just needed to fill my stomach—the way you move into empty houses." She leaned forward. "Hey, dude, why the cool shades on a winter's night?"

"My sunglasses? I'm going to a Halloween party."

"Hey, today isn't Halloween."

Joe laughed lightly. "It isn't? Oh, my!"

Amanda gazed at Joe with growing excitement. "Joe," she said, "I'm on to you. This isn't your house and you're wearing dark glasses. You want to know what I think? You're a thief."

"Mandy, what I am is a professional re-user. I help people by relieving them of things that they aren't using. Then I put the things to good use. By selling them."

Amanda studied Joe's face intently. "Do you ask their permission to take them?" she asked. She liked his cool expression. It didn't give anything away.

"Usually they're sleeping. You know how it is. People need their sleep. I don't like to wake them."

"Oh, man, that's awesome!" Amanda cried with glee. "I've always wanted to meet a real, live thief."

"Why?" asked Joe.

"Because raccoons are always being accused of being thieves. But you're the real thing. Like, way out of here! Joe, are you new to Boulder?"

"Just arrived," he admitted.

"Baby," Amanda assured him, "you're going to love it. Totally. What do you say to our working together?"

"No reason to."

"Sure there is. If you teach me your tricks I'll show you around town. I'll point out some sweet places where people have killer things. You see, Joe," she said slyly, "I think, like, I could help you big time."

"How?"

Amanda grinned. "Trust me. You're big. I'm small. I can get in through chimneys, windows, and holes."

Joe considered Amanda in a new way. Though he didn't think she was too bright, perhaps she could help him in his work. "What about your mother and brother?" he asked.

"Oh, you can chill about them. My ma's so old all she does is sleep. And Philip's a total wuss."

"But Mandy," Joe asked, "can I really trust you?"

"Joe," Amanda said, putting her paw upon her heart, "we two could be the most awesome partners in the world. Right?"

Joe held out his hand. Amanda put her paw in it. They shook. It was a deal.

[NEXT WEEK: PHILIP GOES HOME]

Chapter Five

PHILIP GOES HOME

Sitting in the snow before the house, hot tears running down his white muzzle, chin sore, Philip waited for his sister Amanda to emerge. But though the house lights went off one by one, there was no sign of her.

Quite certain that Amanda was in terrible danger, Philip moaned. He had to do something, but what? Leaving a long, lonely trail of black paw prints in the snow, he started for home, wretched with a sense of his own helplessness and failure.

For Philip, home was the Denver & Rio Grande train that sat in Central Park. The train—Number 30—was a relic of times past. It consisted of an old locomotive and coal tender, passenger car, and caboose. Though the train was on tracks, for years it had gone nowhere.

Philip headed for the caboose—once the dormitory

for the train's crew. He walked behind the front wheels where there was a hole in the floor of the car. After hauling himself up, he walked along the chilly, dark interior until he reached a ladder. The ladder led to the cupola where brakemen once kept watchful eyes on the train. Now Philip lived there with his sister and their mother.

"Who's there?" came a sleepy voice.

"It me, Ma," Philip replied woefully.

Philip's mother—Gloria by name—lay curled up on a bed of leaves. She was a large, shaggy raccoon, with droopy eyes, a thin tail, and mostly all gray fur. "Have a good time?" she asked. She spoke in a very tired voice.

"Not really," Philip mumbled.

"Well, never mind. As long as you ate something. Is Amanda there with you?"

Philip hesitated. Then he said, "Well . . . no."

Gloria looked around. "Why, where is she?"

Philip rubbed his paws nervously.

Slowly, trying to ignore her aches and pains, Gloria roused herself. Over the years she had been mother to fifty-three children. Almost all had grown and moved on. It was her greatest pride that only a few had been lost. "Philip," she demanded, "where is your sister?"

"Ma," he muttered, "something awful happened."

Fully awake now, Gloria shook away leaf bits from her face. She gazed into Philip's unhappy face. "Philip, I need to know about your sister."

Philip told the story. By the time he was done, he

was sobbing. "Do you think that man will hurt her?" he asked, sniffing.

"I don't know," Gloria replied, worrying her paws.

"What's going to happen to her?" Philip wailed.

Gloria reached out and gave Philip's face a pat. "You know Amanda," she said. "If it's not one thing it's another. She knew it was foolish to go in there."

"I should have kept her out," Philip said. "Now I have to help her."

"That's generous of you," Gloria replied. "But how?"

"That's just it," Philip admitted sadly. "I can't think of a way. Can you?"

His mother shook her head. "Son, years ago your dad and I used to ride this train. We traveled all over the West and never knew where we were going next. I suppose you've heard so many stories about it you could drive this train yourself. But even a train has to stop sometime. We stopped with it right here in Boulder. Then, not long after, your dad passed on." Gloria paused to look at the wall where the engineer's cap and red bandanna her husband had worn still hung.

"But, Philip," Gloria went on, "the truth is, I'm tired. Over the years I've rescued too many cubs. I'm all steamed out."

"But Ma, I can't just leave her there!"

"Amanda's clever," Gloria mused. "Maybe she can solve her own problems. As for you, you need to get some sleep."

"I'll never sleep again," Philip announced morosely.

"Of course you will." Gloria shuffled back to her leafy bed. "Come over here and try," she called.

"I don't want to," Philip replied.

Tired though he was, Philip could not sleep. Instead, he sat by the cupola window and stared out at the park. Beneath the full moon, the thin covering of snow glistened as if it were silver dust. In contrast, the trees reminded him of the bars of a cage. "Oh, Amanda," Philip sighed, "what will happen to you?"

[NEXT WEEK: PHILIP TO THE RESCUE]

Chapter Six

PHILIP TO THE RESCUE

The next night Philip headed back to the Grove Street house. When he saw that the window through which they had entered before was closed, he remembered there was a chimney. In minutes he climbed the pine tree and reached the roof.

He stared down the chimney flue. No bottom was in sight. Nonetheless he edged forward and crawled deep into the darkness. Down he went, heart thumping, thoughts filled with all kinds of possible disaster. When he banged his head against something hard, he quickly put out a paw, and felt a flat piece of metal. He lowered himself onto it carefully. Unexpectedly, the metal plate swung down. With a loud plop, Philip tumbled into a fireplace.

He looked into the room. No one was there. Warily,

he inched forward and sniffed, hoping to pick up his sister's scent. Only when he reached the kitchen did he catch a whiff of her. "Amanda!" he called softly. *"Amanda!"* There was no answer.

Philip crept into the bathroom and peered beneath the tub as well as behind the toilet. No Amanda. Finally, he looked in the tub. There she lay, curled up beneath a wool blanket, head on a pillow, fast asleep.

"Amanda!" he whispered. "It's me, Philip!"

Amanda opened her eyes halfway. "Oh, hi, baby. What's happening?"

"Are you all right?" Philip asked.

"My right paw is a little sore, but it was worth it."

"What do you mean? What's worth it?"

"I got to meet Joe."

"Who's Joe?"

"The fellow who's staying here. Philip, he was so cool about what happened, apologizing and fixing my paw. Then we got to talking and Philip, guess what?" Her eyes grew bright with excitement. "Joe is a professional re-user."

"I never heard of that."

"He takes things from houses that people aren't using."

"What?" Philip squeaked.

"Joe sells the stuff and uses the money to take care of himself. It's a useful, responsible, and thrilling life."

"Useful? Thrilling? Amanda! You're talking about a thief!"

"Philip, you are such a nerd. The thing is, Joe's going

to teach me about what he does in exchange for my showing him around town."

"But . . . that would be awful!" Philip cried.

Amanda rolled her eyes. "Philip," she said, "I can totally understand where you're coming from, but it's perfectly obvious you will never understand me."

"He must be forcing you to do this," Philip insisted.

"Philip," Amanda replied, "I want to experience life, not eat and sleep all day the way you do. Face it," she said, "I'm no longer a child."

"Amanda, we're the same age!"

"No way. Listen here, dude, since the last time we spoke I've matured a lot. I'm like a million, billion miles ahead of you in knowing what life is all about. Like, dude, all you do is just sit around and go nowhere, like that train we live on. Well, I'm moving fast. Totally. You can just watch my moves!"

A shocked Philip stared at Amanda. Was this his twin sister talking? He started to say something, only to think better of it. Instead he turned away and left the house the same way he came in, by the chimney.

Perhaps, he hoped, she would quickly come to her senses on her own.

Three nights later a sad Philip was strolling through the park when he noticed a newspaper on the ground. A headline caught his attention:

Boulder Police Chief Baf ed by Night of Break-ins
How did thief get inside? Police Wonder

A rash of house thefts occurred in town last night. Somehow a thief is managing to unlatch doors from the inside. "It's almost as if the thief was small enough to go down chimneys, and through barely open windows," Police Officer Muttonwood said.

When Philip read the story he felt quite ill. He was certain Amanda was involved. But at the same time, he could not believe she was so wrong-headed as to rob people's houses.

"That man is making her do bad things," he said.

Off he rushed to share the news with his mother. Gloria looked at the paper grimly. From time to time she sighed and even growled.

"Oh, Ma," said Philip, "it's that human, Joe. I'll bet you anything he's making her steal! It's all his fault."

Upset as she was, Gloria shook her head. "Philip, I know she's your twin sister, but from all you've said, and from what I know about Amanda, I'm afraid this is her choice."

"Don't you have any faith in her?" Philip protested.

"I'm afraid I don't," Gloria said with a sigh.

"All right," said Philip. "Then I'll prove she's innocent!"

[NEXT WEEK: AMANDA AND JOE]

THE STORY SO FAR:

AMANDA HAS ENTERED INTO A PARTNERSHIP WITH JOE,
THE THIEF SHE MET IN THE GROVE STREET HOUSE.

Chapter Seven

AMANDA AND JOE

It was late at night. Boulder's streets were empty save for a fancy black car moving silently. Behind the wheel sat Joe. Next to him, an excited Amanda bounced up and down.

"That place looks cool," she cried, pointing to a large building. "I say we rob that one."

"That's the Boulder Police Station," Joe informed her.

"That's cool."

"No way!"

Joe drove on a few more blocks.

"Stop!" cried Amanda. "There's sweet stuff in there."

Joe brought the car to a halt in front of a modest house. He studied it carefully. "Might do," he said. "Let's have a look." Large plastic bag in hand, he

stepped out of the car. Amanda, holding a smaller bag, headed right for the house. "Come on!" she called, "What are you waiting for?"

"Mandy, to be successful, a thief has to be careful."

"Oh man, you sound just like my brother," Amanda said, and scampered along. Joe followed hastily. The door was locked. Next to it was a partially open window.

"Okay," said Amanda, "like before, you lift me up and help me through the window. Soon as I get inside I'll open the door for you. Think you can do it, dude?"

"Mandy . . ."

"Chill, baby, chill."

Joe picked Amanda up and set her by the window. She slipped inside. "Now get to the door fast!" Joe called to her. He went back to the front door and waited.

When the door didn't open immediately he put his ear against it. There was a crash inside. He ran back to the window. "What's happening?" he cried softly.

"I knew this place would be cool," Amanda called back. "They've got some wicked garbage."

"Forget the garbage!" Joe cried. "Get the door open."

The door opened. In Amanda's paw was a bit of broken plastic.

"What's that?" Joe asked.

"It's a piece of a toy. Has a sweet shape, don't you think?"

"See here, Mandy," Joe cried. "You don't seem to understand, a real thief isn't interested in junk."

"It's not junk," Amanda said indignantly. "Shapes can be like, very interesting."

"Then wait here," Joe said. "I'm going to search around for some decent things."

"Do what you want, dude," Amanda growled.

Joe crept away, leaving Amanda alone in the kitchen. She looked about. It was a nice room, lined with cabinets, a stove, and a refrigerator. A round table with two chairs sat in one corner. On the ceiling was a fan. But what really caught her interest was a jar of peanut butter on top of the refrigerator. Just seeing it made her mouth water. "Awesome," she whispered.

In haste, she pushed one of the chairs close to the refrigerator and climbed up its ladder back and onto a counter. From there she took a jump, missed, jumped again, and managed to get her claws over the top edge of the fridge. Kicking madly—leaving many scratches on the white metal surface—she pulled herself up atop the refrigerator.

She sat down with the peanut butter jar between her knees and unscrewed the top. She began to scoop out peanut butter in great gobs and stuff it into her mouth.

"Mandy!" called Joe from the other room. "Come here!"

Amanda, speaking with a full mouth, said, "Harumpful."

"What?"

"Harugarklpf."

Joe hurried into the kitchen. His bag was empty. "What did you say? Where are you?"

"Imeatin' 'ool 'eanututter."

"Come on! You said there were some good things here. I can't find anything."

" 'Usta minute," Amanda said and cleared her mouth. "Hey, Joe, there's a funny little switch here. . . ."

"Mandy, don't!" He was too late. Amanda flipped the switch. A burglar alarm began to honk loudly. Within moments a police siren wailed in the distance.

"Forget it!" Joe cried. "We better get out of here!" With that he ran out the door. Amanda was right behind him.

[NEXT WEEK: PHILIP LEARNS THE TRUTH ABOUT AMANDA]

THE STORY SO FAR:

PHILIP, FEARFUL THAT HIS TWIN SISTER HAS BEEN
FORCED INTO A LIFE OF CRIME, TRIES TO HELP HER.

Chapter Eight

PHILIP LEARNS THE TRUTH ABOUT AMANDA

It was two in the morning. Boulder's snowy streets were deserted. Not a moving car was in sight. A hunched-up, shivering Philip sat across from the house on Grove Street. He was convinced that his sister had been forced against her will to become a thief. True, she had told him otherwise, but Philip refused to believe her. As far as he was concerned it was all Joe's fault.

He gazed up at the roof. He was just about to cross the street, go down the chimney, and console his captive sister when a black car swung onto the street and stopped before the house. A man got out of the car. From the sunglasses it was easy to recognize Joe. Philip growled under his breath. He hated the man.

Joe reached back inside the car and hauled out a heavy sack. "Come on, Mandy," Philip heard him say. "I'd really like to get some sleep."

Philip was wondering who Mandy was when he heard a voice say, "Hey, Joe, chill. Like, my feet are beat."

The voice was Amanda's. Sure enough, the next moment Philip saw his sister climb out of the car. He looked for the chain that he assumed would be around her neck, letting the man restrain her. But there was no chain. Amanda was absolutely free.

Philip was about to shout "Amanda, run for it!" when he saw his sister reach into the car and remove her own small sack. He even heard her say, "Just remember, Joe, my paw's still sore where you bopped it."

"Please, Mandy," said Joe, "how many times do I have to apologize? I thought we were done with all that." He opened the door to the house. Amanda, struggling under the weight of her sack, followed.

Philip dashed across the street and peered in through the front window. Joe was rapidly pulling things from his large bag: a clock, a small framed picture, some silverware, a radio, plus a lot more. A shocked Philip realized it was all stolen goods.

Then Amanda began to empty her bag. Out came a crushed can of soda, a bent spoon, a pencil stub, and finally a silk nightgown, slightly torn. When each object appeared she laughed with glee.

Philip's heart sank. "He's really forced my sister to become a thief," he moaned.

Half an hour later the house's lights went out. Philip made his way to the roof and crawled down the chimney as he had done before.

Once he was inside the house, Philip headed right

for the bathroom and peered into the bathtub. There, tucked beneath the blanket, dressed in the torn silk nightgown with a new frilly pillow under her head, lay Amanda, fast asleep.

"Psst! Hey, Amanda, wake up! It's me, Philip."

Amanda opened her eyes, saw who was there, and closed them again. "Go away," she murmured, rolling over.

"Amanda," Philip called, "I've come to rescue you."

"Rescue me? No way," she mumbled. "I'm having fun."

"Come on, Amanda," Philip pressed. "I think that man's sleeping. You can escape through the chimney."

Amanda yawned. "Philip, I wish you'd stop lecturing me. Joe's cool. Like I told you before, he isn't keeping me here."

"But, Amanda . . ."

"Hey, dude, face it. I'm not the sister you knew."

"What do you mean?"

Amanda sat up, looked at Philip, and yawned. "I told you I wanted an exciting life. Well, now I've got a cool one. Like, totally. I'm a real burglar. Tell you what, Philip, I'll make you a deal: You do something to surprise me. Then I'll listen to you. Know what I'm saying?" She plopped down and closed her eyes. "But, like, you won't."

Philip turned away. Not only did he have no idea how to surprise Amanda, he had not the slightest idea how he could rescue her from her plight. As far as Philip was concerned, his sister was doomed.

[NEXT WEEK: PHILIP MAKES A DECISION]

BOULDER POLICE
CHIEF BAFFLED BY
NIGHT OF BREAK-INS

THE STORY SO FAR:

PHILIP, HORRIFIED THAT HIS SISTER HAS BECOME
A THIEF, IS FULL OF DESPAIR.

Chapter Nine

PHILIP MAKES A DECISION

Philip was a deeply upset raccoon. There was no way
he could deny the truth anymore: His sister, Amanda,
had become a thief.

But then, as he dragged himself back toward the train
in Central Park, he stopped in his tracks. If she *was* a
crook, shouldn't he tell the legal authorities what she
was doing? Perhaps they were the only ones who could
keep her from thievery.

The town's courthouse was just a short way up the
creek on Sixth Street. It would take only moments to
reach it. Philip wondered if anyone there would even
listen to him. He was very young. And would they even
pay attention to a raccoon?

Oh, why, Philip berated himself, *can't I think of anything to do?* With some bitterness, he remembered

41

Amanda's words: "You do something to surprise me. Then I'll listen to you." *Amanda is right*, Philip thought, *I don't know how to do anything!*

He shook his head. Perhaps it would be best to keep his mouth shut and tell no one what was happening. The only ones who would know the truth would be himself and his mother. Amanda would be their secret shame. Life—albeit a sad one—would go on.

It was almost dawn when Philip reached the train caboose. There he paused, reluctant to go inside. His mother would ask him hard questions he didn't want to answer. Besides, he was very hungry.

So, instead of going to bed Philip waddled about Central Park looking for food. In time he made his way down to Boulder Creek. The water was high and bubbling, tumbling over rocks, splashing into deep pools. Taking up a position at the very edge of the creek, he put one paw in the icy cold mud and began to feel around for something to eat with his sensitive fingers. Finding nothing, he moved over to a quiet pool where he could wait, watch, and catch a small fish.

A noise from across the creek made him look up. It was Miss Matilda, the deer, one of his mother's friends. Her legs were spread wide, enabling her to bend her neck and lap up the water.

Though Philip did not wish to be impolite, he resolved not to talk. Instead, he pretended to concentrate on a fish which was slowly swimming in his direction.

"How do, Philip," Matilda called from across the creek.

Philip had to look up. "Oh, Miss Matilda! Hello. I didn't see you."

"Dreadful news about Amanda," the deer said softly.

"Oh?" was all Philip could bring himself to say.

"Life in this town," the deer said, "has enough problems without one of us becoming a thief. She'll make all of us animals look bad."

Philip made a snatch at a little fish, but was so rattled by the deer's words he missed. When he looked up Miss Matilda had gone.

More upset than ever, Philip trundled back toward the caboose. A white cat named Pickwick peeked out from a bush. "Ssst, Philip. That sister of yours. She's giving the whole neighborhood a bad name."

Philip, who normally enjoyed playing with Pickwick, hurried on faster than ever.

Just as he reached the caboose, a squirrel by the name of David shouted down from a high wire: "Hey, Philip! What's going to happen to the rest of us animals when the people in town learn your sister's been breaking into houses and stealing their things? Hey! What about the rest of us?"

Philip slunk into the caboose. The entire neighborhood knew about Amanda and what she was doing. What's more, her actions were giving the animal community a bad name. Philip sighed. He would have to accept his responsibility. That meant going to the courthouse to find help for Amanda. No matter what the consequences.

Should I tell Ma? he asked himself.

"No," he said out loud. "I didn't stop Amanda from going into that house. It's my responsibility—and mine alone—to do something."

[NEXT WEEK: PHILIP GOES FOR HELP]

THE STORY SO FAR:

HIS SISTER HAS BECOME A THIEF, SO PHILIP DECIDES TO
GO TO THE BOULDER COURTHOUSE TO SEEK HELP IN
GETTING HER TO STOP.

Chapter Ten

PHILIP GOES FOR HELP

Next morning a jittery Philip waddled slowly along the Boulder Creek jogging trail toward the courthouse. Stalling for time, he paused to fish in the shallow pools by the tumbling water. Though he caught nothing, a new thought crept into his mind: *What if Amanda was sent to jail?* How awful! And it would be his fault! All the same, he felt that for the sake of the park animals he must get help. And Amanda needed help, too. She was in serious trouble, but she didn't even know it. And that, Philip knew, was the worst kind of trouble to be in.

Upon reaching the courthouse, he became even more cautious. Whom should he speak to? A policeman? A lawyer? A judge? And how would he get inside? In vain he scanned the courthouse roof for a chimney. There was none.

Some people standing by the main door were so im-

mersed in a conversation that they paid scant attention to Philip as he stood trying to figure out how to get inside. Then an old lady with a long, tentlike coat approached. She was walking so slowly Philip was able to dart under her coat. Concealed, he walked along with her into the building. No one noticed him.

Once inside, Philip peeked out from under the lady's coat. Seeing no one, he dashed from his hiding place and crept behind a water cooler.

It took a while for his heart to quiet. Then he took a peek about. The courthouse corridors were hushed and deserted. On the walls were signs directing people to courtrooms. *Ah!* Philip thought. *I'll go to a judge. They're supposed to be fair-minded.*

Silently, the young raccoon padded into the first courtroom he came to. It was almost entirely filled with benches. Its walls were paneled with fine wood. The lighting was soft. At first it seemed as if no one was there.

Then Philip saw a small, red-faced man in a black robe seated high up behind a desk at the front of the room. He had a flat, pug nose; hard, beady eyes; and frowning lips.

"May I help you?" he inquired sharply.

Philip, thinking that it was he who was being spoken to, nearly fainted. Then he realized the judge was talking to a man in a police uniform.

"Judge Peebles," said the policeman, "we've got a problem in town."

"Approach the bench," Judge Peebles replied solemnly, "and state your name."

"Police Chief Banyan."

47

"Very well, Chief. You may address the court."

"Judge Peebles, it's this rash of thefts we've been experiencing. Evidence suggests that they are being committed by some of the park animals."

"What kind of evidence?"

"Claw scratches around the break-in sites. Dirty paw marks."

The judge scowled. "Humph! No surprise," he said. "Most animals are thieves. They don't like to work for a living. Now cows and horses, they work. The rest are always expecting handouts. As far as I'm concerned the only good animal is a hunted animal."

"Your Honor, I'm afraid I have to agree with you," replied Chief Banyan.

"Fine! Good!" said the judge. "What do *you* intend to do about it?"

"The police request the court's permission to get rid of the wild animals in the parks. We can gather them all up, take them to the high mountains, and dump them there. Aside from ending the thefts, it would make the parks a lot nicer and a lot cleaner."

"Good idea," agreed Judge Peebles. "If you need the court's permission to do so, it's hereby granted." He banged his gavel.

Philip waited till both the judge and the police chief left the room. Then he fairly flew from the courthouse. What did he care if he was seen? His animal friends were in trouble. Big trouble! Something had to be done.

[NEXT WEEK: SOME ADVICE IS GIVEN]

Chapter Eleven

SOME ADVICE IS GIVEN

Philip was so alarmed by the police chief's words, and by what Judge Peebles had given the police permission to do, that he stayed very close to the caboose for two days.

He did tell his mother about his trip to court. It was too much to keep to himself. "Everybody's in trouble," he said. "And it's all Amanda's fault. I still don't know what to do about her. I'm really desperate," he admitted. "I almost wish I'd never known about any of this stuff."

"It's better that you found out," Gloria said, to comfort her son. "I guess that judge just doesn't care for animals."

Philip nodded sadly. "But that makes it even more important that we do something to save Amanda. Maybe we can show that judge we're not all bad."

49

"Philip," said Gloria with a shake of her head, "you've done the best you can. Amanda is her own raccoon. So are you. As for the other animals, perhaps together you can come up with something. I'm afraid I'm too tired to think." With that she went off to her bed, leaving Philip in tears.

During the next few nights Philip clung to the shadows whenever he went out, eating only the food he could find quickly, bits of candy, a worm or two, a couple of crawfish from the creek. It was not just the town's police he feared. Remembering the words of Miss Matilda the deer, Pickwick the cat, and David the squirrel, he was sure the park animals were angry at him and his mother, as well as Amanda. He was afraid to face them.

But Philip did search for discarded Boulder newspapers. They were full of stories about more robberies. Philip had little doubt: Amanda and her friend were still stealing. It would only be a matter of time before the police did something drastic.

On the third night after Philip had gone to court, he was so hungry he decided he simply had to go down to the creek and do some real fishing. He was about to cross the bike path when he heard some humans talking.

"We've got new orders," a voice was saying, "about the park animals."

Philip crept forward to see who had spoken. Peering through the bushes he saw two Boulder police officers leaning on their bicycles and chatting.

"What orders?" asked the second officer.

"From Chief Banyan. Seems Judge Peebles has agreed to let us go after the wild animals in the park. The evidence suggests they're behind the wave of robberies we've been having."

The second officer shook his head. "And I thought it was just the tourists who were a headache."

"Anyway," the first police officer continued, "if the animals can't behave, the judge says the chief has permission to clear them out. I've heard that Judge Peebles really hates animals."

"I suppose," the second policeman grumbled, "if the park animals get out of hand we have to do something."

The two officers chatted a bit more before cycling off.

Philip was very frightened. What was he to do? If he stayed he'd be rounded up and brought to the high mountains. But even before that, if the animals got wind of what was about to happen, they might turn on him. Maybe it would be better to get away first and fast. The more Philip thought about it, the more that notion appealed to him. It was not long before he made up his mind to leave town. As fast as he could, he scampered home.

To his relief, though not his surprise, his mother was asleep. Quickly, he packed up some belongings in a backpack, then scribbled a note:

Dear Ma: I can't take the pressure. I'm heading for the mountains. I promise to let you know where I settle and you can come join me.

Love, Philip

Backpack in place, Philip headed off in a westerly direction, toward the mountains. Taking the canyon path, he had gone barely a quarter of a mile when he heard a rustle among the bushes. Suddenly, a voice from the dark called: "Hey, pal! Where do you think you're going?"

[NEXT WEEK: THE VOICE FROM THE DARK]

THE STORY SO FAR:

WHEN HIS SISTER'S LIFE OF CRIME MAKES LIFE TOO
DIFFICULT FOR PHILIP, THE YOUNG RACCOON RUNS
AWAY, ONLY TO BE STOPPED BY A VOICE FROM THE DARK.

Chapter Twelve

THE VOICE FROM THE DARK

Startled by the voice, Philip came to a quick stop. He
looked around. There was nothing to see but bushes.
All was dim and still.

"Hey, pal! Over here." A floating white line began to
emerge. Then two black eyes came into view, followed by a
sharp, pointy face. Suddenly, Philip realized it was Hubert,
a skunk his own age. Smaller than Philip, Hubert was black
save for a white stripe along his back and bushy tail.

Philip's fear melted. "Oh, hi," he said, unable to dis-
guise his weariness.

"Hey, pal," said Hubert, "what's the backpack for?"

Unable to admit the truth, even to a friend, Philip
said, "Going camping."

"Want some company?" Hubert asked.

Philip shrugged. "I'm not in the mood and I—" He

stopped, realizing he *did* feel like talking, and that Hubert would be a good listener. "Sure, come along."

As they walked to the creek bank Hubert chatted breezily about happenings in the park, how one family of squirrels was feuding with another family of squirrels, how some ducks found a whole bag of peanuts, how Pickwick the cat was chased by Gibby the dog, and so forth. Philip listened with only half an ear.

At the creek Philip felt obliged to make his way to a quiet pool to watch for fish. Hubert stayed close.

For a while the young raccoon just stared into the cold, dark water. No fish came along. He sighed. He was tired of faking. "I supposed you know all about Amanda," he said softly.

"Oh, sure," Hubert said. "Everyone knows. That Amanda is pretty wild. Remember when she got some Rollerblades and tried to organize daily races at the mall?"

"Yeah, it all stinks," Philip said morosely.

Hubert looked around sharply. His black-and-white plumed tail stood straight up. "What did you say?"

Philip, realizing his blunder, quickly said, "I mean, it's not good."

"That's what I thought you said," Hubert said graciously.

"What I meant is," Philip said, "she's a big problem."

"She'll probably get worse, too," Hubert offered. "One of these nights, she's going to be nabbed. That means big trouble for everyone. They'll really crack down on all of us then."

Philip winced. With a sob, he turned to his friend. "Hubert, I've been trying to figure out what to do. I even went to the courthouse for help. I learned there that Judge Peebles gave permission to the police to kick *all* of us animals out of the park, and . . . it's because of Amanda.

"And that judge meant business, Hubert. Why, just now, I overheard two police officers talking about doing exactly that! So I've pretty well given up. Fact is, I'm running off to the mountains."

"Listen here, pal," said Hubert, "this is too big for you to handle alone."

"What do you mean?"

"If the people in this town get to thinking we animals are a bunch of thieves, we're going to have some rough knocks. Know what I'm saying? Look here, you've been trying to help Amanda by yourself. But the park animals aren't happy either. They all know about her."

"I know," said Philip.

"So what we need to do is get the animals in the park together. Have a meeting."

"A meeting!"

"Maybe together we can think of something."

"Hubert, do you think anyone would even come?"

"Are you kidding, pal?" Hubert said. "Listen here, half-a-dozen animals asked me to get you to call a meeting."

"They did?"

"Pal, they want something done. Fast. And you're the one that has to do it. Amanda is your sister. What do you say?"

"Hubert, I'll try anything."

[NEXT WEEK: PHILIP TRIES TO ORGANIZE A MEETING]

Chapter Thirteen

PHILIP TRIES TO ORGANIZE A MEETING

Having accepted Hubert's idea of holding a general meeting of all the park animals to deal with Amanda, Philip set out immediately to speak to as many of them as he could.

When he went to talk to a pair of geese, they spoke the same words in unison.

"Amanda? Amanda?" they said. "Who's she? Who's she?"

"She's my twin sister," Philip explained, "and she's making trouble for all of us."

"How's that? How's that?"

"She's become a thief, working with a man. They're stealing from Boulder homes."

"Very bad. Very bad," the geese said in unison.

"And," Philip continued, "we're going to hold a gen-

eral meeting tomorrow night at the amphitheater. It's to figure out what to do. Will you come?"

"Well, maybe. Well, maybe," the geese replied.

Gibby, the stray dog, was thrilled. "I *love* meetings!" he yapped. "Lots of friends! Lots of interesting talk! Lots of excitement! Oh, sure! Can't wait! You can count me in! You bet!"

Next Philip came upon Sam, a red fox who usually kept himself somewhat aloof. When he told Sam about the meeting, the fox replied in a shy voice, "Yes, I'd like to come. Perhaps I can be useful."

The rabbits were more cautious. "Well, I don't know," said one. "Ask him," said another. "I'll go if she goes," said a third. All in all Philip was left with the impression that at least some rabbits might be there.

As for the squirrels, they already knew about the meeting. Before he could say anything, they informed him that they would *all* be there. Philip was almost sorry to hear that.

The animal Philip was most nervous about meeting was the coyote, Rebecca. Not only did she have squinty eyes, she had a fixed smile which the young raccoon did not entirely trust.

He found her sitting under the Sixth Street Bridge. A mural of coyotes was there, and Rebecca, who had posed for the artist, never tired of admiring her own image.

"Your sister?" Rebecca said softly. Her pale eyes were fixed on her portrait. "Last I heard she was trying to dam the creek to make a hockey rink."

"That only lasted a week," Philip said, feeling the need to be very respectful. "This is much more difficult."

"What kind of difficult?" Rebecca said, with a wide smile that showed her sharp teeth and red tongue.

Philip retreated a step, then related all that had happened. He concluded by saying, "We need to find a way to rescue my sister before she does a lot of damage—to herself and the rest of us."

"A thief, eh?" murmured Rebecca. "And working with a human. Not smart. Not wise."

"Do you think you could be at the meeting?" Philip asked. "We need to find a way to stop her."

Rebecca stared at her portrait for a long while. At last she said, "Yes, I think so. I might come up with an idea to impress your sister. I just might." She smiled, turned, and trotted away silently.

After speaking to as many animals as he could find, Philip went home and told his mother about the meeting.

"I suppose it's a good notion," Gloria said, "though I'm not sure anyone can change your sister's mind. I suspect you'll need to do something forceful."

"But what?" Philip said. Ruefully, he remembered what Amanda had said: "Philip, I'll make you a deal: You do something to surprise me. Then I'll listen to you. Know what I'm saying?"

Philip could not sleep for trying to think what to do. All night he tossed and turned. Then, in the middle of the night, an idea came to him. Full of excitement, he sat up. "Yes," he thought, "that might be just the thing to surprise Amanda!"

[NEXT WEEK: PHILIP'S SURPRISE]

THE STORY SO FAR:

BECAUSE OF THE PROBLEMS AMANDA HAS CAUSED THE
PARK ANIMALS, PHILIP ORGANIZES A GENERAL
MEETING TO DECIDE WHAT TO DO ABOUT HER.

Chapter Fourteen

PHILIP'S SURPRISE

It was two in the morning. The park animals had gathered on the wooden seats set before the amphitheater. The band shell, painted rainbow colors, glowed in the cold moonlight.

In the front row sat a gaggle of geese, plus a few ducks. The rabbits kept under the benches. Miss Matilda the deer had come—along with her companion, a dignified, older-looking stag. Gibby, the dog, went rushing about licking as many faces as he could, much to the animals' annoyance. Pickwick brought along a whole packet of cats, all friends. Sam the fox was there, too, as well as a host of raccoons, Philip's many relations. As for Rebecca the coyote, she lay stretched out, tongue lolling, a hungry look on her face.

Of course Philip was there with Hubert, the skunk. They were sitting in the first row.

"I'm a little nervous," Philip confessed, worrying his paws.

"Of course you are."

"Hubert, don't you think I'm a little too young to be holding a meeting?" He stole a glance over his shoulder. "Most of these animals are much older than me."

"Hey, pal, it's your sister, not theirs."

"That's true," Philip said. "I just don't want to look foolish. Amanda always says I'm stupid."

Hubert frowned. "Hey, pal, I'd rather look stupid than *be* stupid. Know what I'm saying?"

"I guess," Philip said, sighing. Slowly, he made his way to the front of the band shell. At first he just stood there saying nothing, merely rubbing his paws together, and wondering where his mother was. When he did see her she was at the far back. She offered a nod of encouragement.

"First off," Philip began, in a voice that sounded a little squeaky to his own ears, "my mom and I want to thank you. We do appreciate your concern about my sister."

Then he proceeded to relate what Amanda had done, and what he feared she would continue to do.

"Do get to the point," suggested Rebecca the coyote. There was a bite of authority in her voice.

"Hey, pal, let the kid tell it his way," Hubert said, with an ominous shake of his tail. Rebecca smiled and showed her teeth but said no more.

Philip continued. "Though my sister has taken up a life of crime, she's really a good sort. Just a little wild."

"I'll say. I'll say," gabbled the geese.

"I went to the courthouse. I heard a judge and the police chief threaten to kick all of us animals out of the park because of what Amanda is doing. They don't know it's her and I'd rather not tell them. But we have to do something. That's what this meeting is about: To see if we can find a way to save her and help ourselves, too."

"Dig a hole," cried one of the squirrels. "Dump her in. Cover her up and forget her. That's what we do with nuts."

"Perhaps a committee might appeal to her better senses," Miss Matilda suggested.

"I don't think she'll listen," Philip said.

Rebecca said: "You said she's robbing homes every night. I say let's catch her in the act of robbery. Then we can bring her back and put her on trial."

"Yes! Yes!" cackled the geese with glee. "Public trial! Public trial!"

The red squirrels promised that if the others caught Amanda they would build a jail cell to hold her.

"But we need to catch her," Gibby barked. "And once we do that we'll have to get her back here."

Philip cleared his throat. "Amanda is my sister," he said. "I might have been a little slow to react, but I think I've got an idea about what to do."

Gloria looked at her son with surprise.

Philip said, "Why not use the park train to nab her?" The crowd of animals gasped.

"But it hasn't run in years!" Hubert the skunk called.

"All the better," Philip replied. "The way to impress Amanda is to do something that will surprise her. The train would be just the thing to shock her into realizing what she's done. As for making it go, my dad and mom rode it for years. I'm sure we could get it moving again.

"With the train we can grab her, then bring her back. Of course, I do need to find out where and when she intends to steal again. But . . . what do you think?"

When the animals burst into applause, Philip grinned with delight.

[NEXT WEEK: WHAT PHILIP SEES AND LEARNS]

THE STORY SO FAR:

THE PARK ANIMALS, HAVING AGREED ON A WAY TO
DEAL WITH AMANDA, SEND PHILIP TO DISCOVER
HER PLANS.

Chapter Fifteen

WHAT PHILIP
SEES AND LEARNS

The next evening Philip returned to the house on
Grove Street. Every light was out. All was still. There
was not even a sign of Joe's car.

Having become adept at working his way to the roof,
crawling down the chimney, and making his way about
the house, Philip did just that. Inside the house, he
found the main room littered with junk— silver foil bits,
bottle caps, a few bent spoons. Philip had no doubt it
was evidence of Amanda's thievery.

But other than an unmade bed in the bathtub, he
detected no sign of his sister. Cautiously, he worked his
way up the spiral staircase, sniffing and listening. He
continued his search on the second floor. He found no
hint of where either Amanda or Joe might be.

Philip was just about to return to the first floor when

he heard the roar of a car racing down the street. With an ear-piercing, squealing shriek it stopped right in front of the house. Alarmed, Philip listened intently.

"Mandy! Be careful," cried Joe.

"Chill, baby, chill," he heard Amanda snap. "There's nothing wrong with my driving."

"But you don't even have a driver's license," Joe cried.

"Hey, dude," Amanda said, "raccoons can't get a drivers' license in Colorado. But I have to drive, right? Like, so totally no big deal. Don't be a nerd, okay? Be cool."

"All right, all right," Joe said. "Let's just get inside. I'm really worn out."

"How about carrying my sack," Amanda said. "It's heavy."

"It's all that garbage you take," Joe murmured.

Philip started down the spiral staircase but barely reached the halfway point when he realized he'd listened too long. Amanda and Joe were already coming into the house.

Crouching on the steps, he watched and waited.

The front door opened. Joe—wearing sunglasses as usual—entered first, carrying two bags. Amanda followed. When Philip saw her, he could hardly believe his eyes.

Not only were Amanda's lips painted deep purple, the white fur on her cheeks had been blushed red. Thick black lines ringed her eyes, while heavy earrings dangled from both ears. The crest of fur on her head

had been spiked and dyed a brilliant kelly green. The green extended in a stripe along her back until it reached her tail, which had turned neon orange. As for the tip of the tail, it was adorned with a ring. On her rear paws she wore heavy, black boots.

As Philip looked on, Joe dumped the contents of his sack onto the floor. There were gilt-edged dishes, candlesticks, and some CDs, as well as a small television.

"Your stuff is *so* dumb," Amanda said. "Do my sack."

"Nothing but trash," Joe insisted.

Amanda rolled her eyes. "You're a wuss," she retorted.

Joe emptied Amanda's loot onto the floor. It consisted of a battered old can of sardines, a bottle cap opener, a bunch of half-eaten carrots, plus a large bag of shiny flip tops from soda cans. "Worthless," Joe said. "When I asked you to go with me I thought you'd have some taste."

"Then let's go to that big house you showed me," Amanda said. "It must have really awesome stuff."

"Are you a fool, Mandy?" cried Joe. "That's Judge Peebles' house, the toughest judge in Boulder County."

"Like, who cares?" Amanda replied. "I mean, what's your problem? If you don't want to go, like, I'll go myself."

"I suppose there would be good things there," Joe admitted, with some uneasiness.

"Cool," said Amanda. "Tomorrow we'll clip the judge."

With great stealth, Philip crawled upstairs and under

Joe's bed. There he waited until Joe had gone to sleep. Convinced Amanda would never listen, Philip did not even bother to speak to her. Instead, he crawled outside through the chimney, then raced toward the park in order to inform the other animals about what he'd heard: Amanda was going to rob *Judge Peebles'* house! It was the worst news ever.

[NEXT WEEK: PHILIP SOUNDS THE ALARM]

THE STORY SO FAR:

PHILIP, HAVING LEARNED THAT HIS SISTER AMANDA
PLANS TO ROB JUDGE PEEBLES' HOUSE, HURRIES BACK
TO INFORM THE PARK ANIMALS.

Chapter Sixteen

PHILIP SOUNDS THE ALARM

Philip ran straight back to Central Park and the old
Denver & Rio Grande Railroad locomotive. Once he
reached it, he climbed into the engine's cab, then
worked his way out the window and along the boiler
side to the old train's warning bell. Grasping the handle, he began to ring it.

Throughout the park the animals heard the clanging.
Within minutes they had gathered at the amphitheater.

"I went to see Amanda to find out her plans," Philip
informed them. "She looks very different, and—"

"Never mind what she *looks* like," said Sam the fox.
"What's she going to do?"

"She—and Joe—are going to rob Judge Peebles'
house."

"Peebles? Peebles?" cried the geese.

"The one who hates animals?" Miss Matilda asked in a voice full of alarm.

"I'm afraid so," Philip said. "Tomorrow night."

Rebecca the Coyote's eyes glowed with anger.

"There's no time to waste," Hubert cried. "We've got to catch Amanda fast and teach her a lesson."

There was a general chorus of approval.

"I really think we should use the locomotive," said Philip. "I know Amanda. It'll make a great impression on her."

Hubert came forward. "All in favor of using the train to rescue Amanda from villainy, bray 'aye.'"

There was a chorus of growls, barks, and squeals of approval.

"Philip," Hubert went on, "do you really know how to drive the train?"

"I've spent my whole life on it," he replied.

"Call 'aye,'" cried Hubert, "if you want Philip to run the train."

Once again the motion was passed.

Philip called Gloria forward and asked her to tell them what they needed to do to get the train ready. With her travels on the train, she knew more than enough. Everyone set to work. Larger animals scurried forth to fetch as many fallen branches as they could find. Smaller ones gathered lots of fire-starting twigs. Squirrels were asked to dig up their nut hoards, since burning nuts give off great heat. They also began constructing a jail cell.

As for the cats, they were sent to see if they could

find a source of fire, while ducks and geese were to make sure the old engine's boiler was filled with water.

Philip asked his mother to inspect the wheels, while the gang of raccoons checked all valves and pistons.

Before the night was over, Engine Number 30 was ready to go. The fire box was stuffed with wood. The boiler was filled with water. All levers and wheels were pronounced in good order, capable of shifting and turning.

All that was wanting was the certainty that Amanda—along with Joe—was truly going to Judge Peebles' house.

The next night, while the rest of the animals stood by the engine in readiness, a pack of cats—under Pickwick's command—surrounded the Grove Street house. Paying no mind to snow flurries, they settled down to wait.

It was about one in the morning when Amanda, clumping loudly in her heavy boots, came out of the house. Her orange tail seemed to be on fire. The green stripe along her back glowed like a twist of rotten cheese. Joe, who looked very unhappy, was with her.

"I'm still not convinced this is a good idea," he said to Amanda as he slipped into his black car. Amanda took the driver's seat.

"Hey, baby, chill," she squawked. "Like, this is going to be the biggest thing to hit Colorado since Pike's Peak."

With tires squealing and smoking, the car roared off.

"Come on!" Pickwick cried. "Back to the train!"

[NEXT WEEK: THE DENVER & RIO GRANDE ROLLS AGAIN!]

THE STORY SO FAR:

THE PARK ANIMALS, WANTING TO NAB AMANDA IN THE
ACT OF STEALING, SET OUT TO CATCH HER WITH THE
OLD PARK TRAIN.

Chapter Seventeen

THE DENVER & RIO GRANDE ROLLS AGAIN!

The locomotive—old Number 30—was alive with energy. The boiler was full of hot water. The fire box—stuffed with wood—was aflame. Twelve raccoons were at hand to feed in more fuel.

At the controls stood Philip. His father's engineer's cap was on his head and the red bandanna was around his neck. With eyes already red with heat and soot, he rested his paws on the brake and power levers. By his side, ready to give advice, was Gloria. The other animals were all over the engine, atop the cab as well as on the boiler.

"They've started for the Judge's house!" cried Pickwick as he raced up to the engine.

Philip reached over his head and pulled the whistle cord. A high, piercing shriek broke through the calm of the cold winter night. Animals clapped paws or wing tips to ears.

"Light the lamps!" Philip called. A squirrel opened the lamp box and flicked the sparker. The train's head lamp burst on, illuminating a swath of track.

"Are we ready?" called Philip.

Atop the engine cab, Rebecca surveyed the animals. "Yes!" she called out.

"All aboard!" Pickwick cried and shifted a lever. The engine, which had not moved for years, creaked and groaned. The fire box blew out a cloud of soot, blackening the faces of the animals in the cab. But the locomotive still did not move.

Philip—along with all the other animals—held his breath as he pushed the power lever higher.

With agonizing squeaks and squeals, the ancient piston rods began to slide. The four huge driving wheels screamed as red rust crumbled away. But the train still did not move.

Philip lifted the power level even higher. The whole locomotive trembled, causing the hair on Philip's neck to prickle. Hubert the skunk was so excited he lifted his tail and sprayed one of the rabbits with his stink. The stench caused the rabbit to faint and fall to the ground, where he lay in a stupor until early the next morning.

Wheezing hot steam, puffing smoke from the stack, the locomotive shook, then let out a deep-throated *chuff!* All eight driving wheels creaked forward half an inch. Out came another *chuff!* spewing sparks in all directions. Chuffing madly, the train began to inch along the tracks.

The animals cheered.

"More wood!" Philip urged.

The soot-blackened raccoons flung on the firewood as fast as they could. The fire blazed. Smoke poured forth. Hot steam hissed. The whistle screamed.

The engine was just picking up speed when it reached the end of the short, curved track section. It lurched to a stop.

"More wood!" Philip shouted. The raccoons worked feverishly, heaving on more fuel. The fire box roared with red hot flames.

Philip pushed the power lever to its highest point. With a jolt—which caused one or two of the small ducks to go flying off the cab—the engine slid off the tracks and onto Broadway.

Once again the animals cheered.

Belching steam, smoke, and sparks, the engine rumbled along Broadway, picking up speed as it went. It reached the Pearl Street Mall and kept on going.

Philip leaned out of the cab window. "What number is Judge Peebles' house?"

"Forty-six Broadway!" cried Pickwick.

Whistle howling, engine puffing black smoke, the locomotive went up a hill. Sam banged the bell. David the squirrel used the headlamp to read the house numbers.

"There's the house," he cried. Parked right in front of it was Joe's black car. No one was in it. Joe and Amanda were already inside the judge's house.

[NEXT WEEK: INTO JUDGE PEEBLES' HOUSE]

79

THE STORY SO FAR:

USING BOULDER'S OLD LOCOMOTIVE, THE ANIMALS RIDE
TO JUDGE PEEBLES' HOUSE IN HOPES OF CATCHING
AMANDA AND BRINGING HER TO JUSTICE.

Chapter Eighteen

INTO JUDGE PEEBLES' HOUSE

Judge Peebles' house was an elegant brownstone structure with a steeply pitched green roof. The porch roof and gables were fringed with fancy woodwork and painted in green, purple, and white. The lights were off. All was quiet.

When the locomotive—oozing steam and smoke—came to a halt, Philip felt more nervous than ever. Leaning out of the cab, he studied the building. All the windows and doors were closed. How would he be able to get in?

Philip noticed a tall chimney on the roof. The moment he saw it, he knew it would be the best way into the house.

He conferred with Hubert and the two quickly agreed upon a plan. Philip would get himself into the house

by going down the chimney. Once inside, he would open any windows or doors leading out. The other animals would be watching the house. As soon as they saw that the house was open, they would swarm inside, find Amanda, and haul her back on the train.

If this doesn't surprise Amanda, Philip thought as he climbed out of the engine, *nothing will.*

"Philip," Gloria cried after him, "keep your eye on Amanda!"

Taking a deep breath, Philip scurried to the front steps and onto the porch. He clawed his way up the wooden posts, which in turn enabled him to scramble up the elegant woodwork on the porch roof, then to the rooftop. In a matter of minutes he had reached the chimney.

Philip looked below. He realized he was much higher than he had been at the Grove Street house. He peered at the train and his friends. They seemed quite small. For a moment he felt dizzy. Then he braced himself. "Don't be a wuss," he told himself. "Get on with it." After checking that there was no fire below, he started down.

Within moments he found himself in a fireplace that looked out into a large room. The ceiling light was on, letting him see that the walls were covered with books about just two subjects: law and hunting.

In one corner of the room was a large, wingback chair. Seated in the chair was Judge Peebles, fast asleep. He was wrapped in his black robe. His legs were stretched forward. His shoes were off, revealing that one of his socks had a big hole. On his lap lay a hunting book. It was titled *The Law of Hunting*. Leaning against the wall, in easy reach, was a shotgun.

Seeing the judge—and his gun—caused Philip's heart to jump. For a second all he wanted to do was scramble back up the chimney and head for the mountains. But when he took another, calmer look he realized that the judge was so deeply asleep that he might, if he was quiet enough, slip by.

Philip searched for the room's door. It was close to the sleeping judge but it was open. Philip crept forward.

Moving on the tips of his claws, he trotted by the judge and found himself in a long hallway. Gazing up and down, he saw nothing to suggest which way to go. Then he spied a large door at the far end. It looked like the main entrance to the house. If he could open it the other animals would be able to get in. He started down the hallway.

Halfway there he heard whispering voices.

"Mandy"—it was Joe's voice—"get out of that medicine cabinet. You're going to fall and wake the judge. A half-used tube of toothpaste just isn't worth taking."

"Hey, dude," came Amanda's retort, "butt out. Know what I'm saying? Like, if I want some striped toothpaste, like, that's my business, not yours. Now give me a lift down."

"Mandy," Joe cried, "I've had it. You can stay there for all I care. We're quits."

"Hey man, you're a total nerd!" Amanda screeched. "A thief in a suit and tie. Get out of my life."

The next moment Philip saw Joe stomp out of the room. This was followed by a great crashing sound.

Amanda began to scream.

Philip whirled and started down the hallway, only to see an angry Judge Peebles burst from the living room. In his hand was the shotgun.

[NEXT WEEK: TRYING TO CATCH AMANDA]

THE STORY SO FAR:

IN HIS EFFORTS TO SAVE AMANDA, PHILIP HAS CRAWLED INTO THE JUDGE'S HOUSE. THE OTHER ANIMALS WAIT OUTSIDE.

Chapter Nineteen

TRYING TO CATCH AMANDA

Philip took one look at Judge Peebles' angry red face and darted into the room from which Amanda's screech had come.

It was a small washroom with a sink, medicine cabinet, and toilet. The top of the toilet tank had been knocked askew. On the floor lay Amanda, dazed. Her purple lips were smeared. The thick black lines around her eyes had begun to run. On her head the spikes of kelly green fur had wilted. The orange tip of her tail was faded. In one of her paws was a tube of toothpaste. The paste—like a long, multicolored noodle—was wrapped around her. She looked up and saw Philip.

"Philip, baby," she murmured, "what's happening?"

"The judge is right outside."

"What judge?"

85

"The man who lives here."

"Killer bummer! I told that dork Joe it was a mistake to come here," Amanda lied. "Where is he?"

"I saw him running down the hall. But—"

"Philip," Amanda moaned, "my head, like, hurts."

Footsteps reverberated in the hallway. "Amanda," urged Philip, "I bet that's the judge. He's looking for you."

Amanda's eyes filled with alarm. "Save me!" she cried.

Philip looked around. There was only room enough for one raccoon to hide behind the door. "The toilet tank," he cried. "You can hide in there."

"But it's full of water . . ."

"Amanda! Do it!" insisted Philip. He grabbed his sister and hauled her up.

She dipped a paw in the water. "It's too cold," she whined.

"Amanda, hurry!"

Muttering objections, Amanda got into the tank, and sank down until only her head was above water. "Philip, this is so—" She never finished.

"Hold your breath!" Philip advised as he slid the toilet tank top back, hiding her. Then he jumped behind the door.

The next moment the door was flung open. Judge Peebles, gun in hand, burst in. He looked about, saw nothing, scowled, then pulled back and slammed the door.

Philip scurried out from behind the door and pushed the toilet tank lid aside. A miserably wet Amanda looked out. All the colors of her hair and makeup had run together. She looked like a finger painting left out in the rain.

"Philip . . ." she said through chattering teeth, "Please get me out of here."

Philip extended a paw. Amanda grasped it and pulled herself out. Rivers of green and orange poured over the floor. Water poured from her boots.

Philip opened the door and peeked out. He saw no one. "Follow me!" he whispered.

Amanda, trailing colored water, followed.

Philip decided the chimney was the best way out. He started to head back to the fireplace only to see the judge at the end of the hall. The shotgun was still in his hand.

"Halt!" the judge shouted.

Philip stopped. Amanda bumped into him. "The other way," Philip cried. "Fast!"

Philip—with Amanda clumping behind in her combat boots—ran up the hallway, searching desperately for a way to escape.

"Stop!" cried the judge.

At the end of the hall Philip tried the front door. It was locked. The raccoons ran into a large dining room. A table and chairs dominated the area. Philip noticed a large window. On each side of the window were grips.

He raced to the window and looked out. The face of Hubert the skunk looked in at him.

"Amanda," Philip called, "help me get the window open."

Philip took hold of one grip, Amanda the other. "Pull," Philip cried.

Outside, other animals had begun to gather. They, too, attempted to lift the window. It refused to budge.

Judge Peebles stormed into the room. "There you are," he cried. Jerking his shotgun up, he pulled the trigger. There was an enormous explosion.

[NEXT WEEK: AFTER THE EXPLOSION]

Chapter Twenty

AFTER THE EXPLOSION

The pellets from the shotgun blast went over Philip's head. Amanda was not so lucky. Most of the green fur on the top of her head was shaved away, leaving her completely bald.

But the shot did hit the window full blast, blowing the glass to smithereens. Fortunately, the animals outside had seen the judge and his gun and had scattered to safety just before the gun went off.

As the smoke cleared, Philip, seeing the window was no longer there, leaped outside. Quickly, he turned back, grabbed hold of Amanda, and tried to pull her along.

"Oh, no you don't," cried the judge. Flinging his gun to one side, he snatched at Amanda but only managed to grasp her boots. Amanda was now being pulled two different ways: toward the outside by Philip, toward the inside by Judge Peebles.

"Help!" Amanda cried. "I'm being split in two!"

It was then that Gloria reached the window. Seeing her daughter's predicament and, moreover, understanding what Philip was doing, she leaned through the window and yanked the bootlace knots. The moment the knots became loose Amanda popped free from her boots and tumbled outside.

The judge, still clinging to Amanda's boots, reeled back the other way. Even as he did, Joe—trying to escape from the house—burst into the room. The judge, all but flying through the air, struck the thief, knocking him flat on his back, and landed right on top of his chest.

The judge looked down at Joe and said, "I'll bet you're the one breaking into all of Boulder's houses. Good! You're under arrest!"

Joe looked up, saw it was the judge, and fainted.

As for Philip, Amanda, and Gloria, they landed in a tangled heap on the front porch. At first, all the animals looking on simply gawked. The next moment, they rushed forward, scooped Amanda up, and carried her to the waiting locomotive. Philip and his mother tumbled after her.

As soon as they got into the cab Philip shoved the power lever down. Steam hissed, smoke billowed, and the whistle shrieked. The old Denver & Rio Grande locomotive let forth a great groan, went into reverse,

and began to rumble back down Broadway, exactly the way it had come.

A dazed, wet Amanda was shoved into a corner and immediately surrounded by a fierce guard of squirrels, raccoons, and rabbits.

"Where are we?" she asked as she looked into the stern faces of her guards.

"You're about to learn a lesson," Hubert informed her.

As the locomotive clattered along, Amanda watched with wide eyes as Philip worked the controls. Becoming excited, she kept trying to jump up to see everything that was happening. It took all her guards' strength to keep her under control.

Upon reaching the corner of Broadway and Canyon the locomotive slipped right back onto its regular tracks, and Philip applied the brakes. Gradually, the train came to a halt, bumping gently into the passenger car, which had never moved. With a massive hiss of steam, the old engine released its steam and settled back down as if to sleep for another forty years.

As soon as the engine stopped, Amanda was grabbed by her animal guards and marched off the train.

"Hey, dudes! Where do you think you're taking me?" she demanded.

"You'll see. You'll see," cried the geese.

With Hubert leading the way and both Philip and Gloria following, Amanda was marched forcibly toward the creek. There, near a bend in the tumbling waters, where thick bushes had grown close to the water, was a small jail cell built of thorny twigs, which had been constructed by the squirrels.

"In she goes!" cried Hubert.

Pickwick held the entryway open and Amanda was thrust inside.

"But, like, what's going to happen to me?" Amanda cried as the entrance was closed and bound shut and Rebecca took up a guard position to keep her from escaping.

"Tomorrow night," Hubert informed her, "you go on trial!"

[NEXT WEEK: AMANDA LEARNS HER FATE]

Chapter Twenty-one

AMANDA LEARNS HER FATE

Twenty-four hours later, on a cold and blustery night, Amanda was brought to trial in the amphitheater. The park animals gathered on the benches. Few were smiling. Amanda, no longer very colorful, and rather cold and miserable with her bald head, was marched to the stage, surrounded by a fierce guard of cats, ducks, and rabbits.

Hubert the skunk, having black fur—save for one white streak—was chosen to be the judge. He looked more like one than anyone else.

Rebecca the coyote was asked to be the prosecutor. But when it came to defending Amanda, no one wanted the job.

Philip stepped forward. "I guess I'll do it," he said. "After all, she is my sister."

A jury of twelve park animals—two squirrels, three

95

raccoons, a couple of cats, Miss Matilda, three rabbits, and Gibby the dog—sat on one side of the stage. Hubert was in the middle.

Hubert banged a stick on the stage. "The trial of Amanda Raccoon begins. She has been charged with thievery. There is a further charge of endangering the community of her friends and family." He looked toward Amanda. "Do you plead guilty or not guilty?"

Amanda lifted her bald head and said, "I mean, like I totally understand where you're coming from," she said tearfully. "But well, you're all so boring. Like, there's nothing to do. So really it's all your fault."

"She pleads not guilty!" Hubert announced. He turned to Rebecca. "State your case."

Rebecca stood up, fixed her smile, plumped her tail, looked at Amanda, looked at the jury, looked at the audience, and said: "Your Honor, this raccoon became a thief. It was her free choice. She was urged not to do so. Told it was wrong. Nonetheless her thievery ended only when she was captured, put in jail, and brought to trial. She must pay for her wrongful acts!"

Hubert banged his stick. "Philip," he said, "what have you to say in your sister's defense?"

Philip came forward slowly. "Well, actually," he began, worrying his paws, "I don't know what I can say to help Amanda. I mean, those things Rebecca said she did, well, she did. I mean, see, she's just a kid. Like me. Full of energy. Know what I'm saying? I just think, like, she doesn't think a lot about what might happen. And . . . also . . ." Philip began, only to stop. He sighed.

"All I'm saying is, my mom and I would just like you to go easy on her."

Amanda, listening, shed large tears.

"Why are you crying?" Hubert demanded.

"It's such a sad story," Amanda wailed. "It makes me feel sorry for myself."

Hubert turned to the jury. "Animals of the jury," he said, "consider and render your verdict!"

The jury members put their heads together with much gabbling, barking, and squeaking.

"Animals of the jury," Hubert asked, "have you reached a verdict?"

"Sure have," Gibby announced. "Amanda is guilty, but since she is young, we think she should be given some mercy."

Hubert banged his stick. "Amanda, rise!" The young raccoon, holding Philip's paw, stood up. "You have been found guilty. You are sentenced as follows: You must return everything you have stolen. And you must work five hours a week for six weeks picking up trash from the park. Otherwise you'll be handed over to Judge Peebles!" He banged his stick. "The trial is over."

Back home in the caboose with Philip and Gloria, Amanda, staring at her feet, said, "Honest, I've learned a lot from this experience. I won't be a thief anymore."

"That's a relief," Philip said. "Now you can settle down."

Amanda smiled. "Well, actually, like I do have to return all those things I stole. And collect that trash. I want to."

"Good for you," Gloria said. "That shows you've learned something from all this."

"I'll say I have," Amanda replied. "I learned a cool way to return the stolen stuff," she said.

"How?" Philip asked, suddenly feeling a little nervous.

"The train, dude. Man, I loved that ride. Loved how you did it. Way cool. See, I'm going to use the train to return all that junk, then take it for a real spin. Think of it, Philip, right down the turnpike to Denver. Know what I'm saying? Like, killer awesome. Out of sight. Totally."

AVI has reached more than nine million readers with his Amanda stories through over eighty newspaper serializations in the United States and Canada. He is the author of *Nothing But the Truth* and *The True Confessions of Charlotte Doyle*, both Newbery Honor Books; *Poppy*, winner of the Boston Globe-Horn Book Award, along with *The True Confessions of Charlotte Doyle*; *Poppy and Rye*; *Beyond the Western Sea*; and many other books. His other awards include the Scott O'Dell Award, the Christopher Medal, and many children's choice awards. Avi lives in Denver, Colorado, and invites readers to visit him at **www.avi-writer.com** on the World Wide Web.

DAVID WISNIEWSKI is the winner of the 1997 Caldecott Medal for *Golem*. His books include *The Secret Knowledge of Grown-ups*, *Elfwyn's Saga*, and *The Warrior and the Wise Man*. He is a former circus clown and has directed the Clarion Shadow Theatre with his wife, Donna. David Wisniewski lives in Maryland.